COY AND RABBIT

A Tale from the Southwest

by Roy Lewis
illustrated by Cathy Shimmen

SCHOOL PUBLISHERS

Printed in China

ISBN 10: 0-15-350682-2
ISBN 13: 978-0-15-350682-6

Ordering Options
ISBN 10: 0-15-350600-8 (Grade 3 On-Level Collection)
ISBN 13: 978-0-15-350600-0 (Grade 3 On-Level Collection)
ISBN 10: 0-15-357903-X (package of 5)
ISBN 13: 978-0-15-357903-5 (package of 5)

4 5 6 7 8 9 10 0940 12 11 10 09

Coyote had many troubles with Rabbit because Rabbit always got the better of him. Coyote was swift, but Rabbit seemed just a bit swifter. Coyote was clever, but Rabbit was more clever. Coyote was stronger, but Rabbit's many cousins always came to his aid.

The more Coyote thought about Rabbit, the angrier he became. "He makes a fool of me," Coyote thought. Coyote decided then and there to get the best of Rabbit once and for all.

The next morning, as Coyote trotted along,
he heard voices and stopped in his tracks.
Hawk and Crow were chatting in the jack pines.

"What an incredible storm last night!"
exclaimed Crow.

"Yes, lightning struck an enormous rock on the
canyon rim," Hawk continued. "The rock fell into
the canyon. You know the opening at the end?"

"Where the stream flows when there is a
big rain?" asked Crow.

4

"Yes, that's the place. It is blocked now," said Hawk. "The rock fell to the bottom, so the opening is closed. It's a box canyon now, so there is only one way out for those without wings."

Suddenly, Hawk turned and said to Coyote, "You need not hide yourself, Coyote, because I've seen you all along."

Coyote was very excited about what he had overheard. He had once chased Rabbit up that canyon, but then Rabbit had made a leap sideways, and he had disappeared through a hole too small for Coyote to get through. Now Coyote could try this again, and this time the small hole would be gone.

The very next day, Coyote leaped from behind a rock as Rabbit tore into the canyon. "Rabbit thinks he will fool me, but this time it will be he who is the fool," thought Coyote smugly.

Coyote's plan worked because when Rabbit ran into the canyon, he did not know the way was blocked. When he came to the place where he had leaped sideways before, there was no way out.

Rabbit looked this way and that, and he saw that there was no longer an escape, but still he sat calmly. "I must praise you, Coyote, because it seems you have been smarter than I," said Rabbit. This remark pleased vain Coyote because he liked to think of himself as wise.

"I have an offer for you," said Rabbit. "It is true that you planned well, yet it was not you who put this rock into my path."

Coyote did not like this thought although he knew it was true.

"Today you will eat by luck, not by your own wisdom. I would like to make you an offer you would be foolish to refuse. If you spare me today, I will teach you our tricks, and then you will be able to catch rabbits whenever you want."

"Why should I let you go?" snickered Coyote.

"Well, you can feed yourself today, or you can learn how to eat well every day," replied Rabbit.

"You will trick me, and you will surely flee," said unsure Coyote.

"No, I will not," Rabbit promised, "and I will show you how we trick you and get away."

"How can I trust someone who has fooled me so many times before?" asked Coyote.

"Rabbit always keeps his word," said Rabbit.

"I accept your offer, so teach me what I must know," decided Coyote.

Rabbit showed Coyote how he could hide in the brush, but Coyote already knew this. Rabbit showed Coyote how he often ran in circles, but Coyote knew this, too. Rabbit showed him how he stopped so quickly that Coyote would just run right past him.

"I have seen these things many times, so show me a trick I don't know," demanded Coyote.

"My best trick is a quick step to the side," said Rabbit. "Try it."

Coyote tried it several times, but could not do it like Rabbit.

"I think the problem is that your eyes are in the wrong place," declared Rabbit.

"There's absolutely nothing wrong with my eyes," said Coyote.

"Not for a Coyote, perhaps," said Rabbit. "I am a rabbit, so my eyes are on the sides of my head, and I see well to the side. Your eyes are in the front of your head, so you cannot see to the side."

"Try turning your head to the side and keeping it there," suggested Rabbit. "Then you will be able to see to jump to the side."

"It's really not very easy," said Coyote.

"Let's practice it a few times," coaxed Rabbit.

Coyote turned his head and tried jumping to the side several times slowly.

"There's not enough space to practice here. Let's get out of the canyon," suggested Rabbit. They climbed out of the canyon and onto the rim.

Coyote and Rabbit practiced. Rabbit jumped sideways, and Coyote jumped with him. Coyote did not like holding his head to the side because he could not see where he was going. Still, he wanted to be able to catch Rabbit at any time.

"Let's try it once more as fast as we can," said Rabbit.

They moved along the edge of the canyon rim. Rabbit ran very fast. Coyote ran after him even faster.

"Get ready!" hollered Rabbit. This time Rabbit did not jump sideways but stopped short. Coyote, who was looking to the side, did not see him. He tripped over Rabbit, fell over the edge of the canyon, and took a long, long fall.

Rabbit peeked over the edge of the canyon. Coyote was lying at the bottom. "You have tricked me again!" shouted Coyote.

"I have kept my word and showed you my tricks," replied Rabbit. "There was just one more, and now you have seen it." Rabbit laughed and ran away.

"Yes, I guess I have," said Coyote.

Coyote still chases Rabbit to this day. When he does, he always holds his head to the front. You may see him move his head quickly from side to side, but he will not leave it there. He is looking forward to a day when he will catch clever Rabbit.

Think Critically

1. What are two reasons that Coyote wants to catch Rabbit?

2. How do you think Coyote felt about being tricked by Rabbit yet again?

3. Why does Rabbit not seem afraid when Coyote corners him?

4. How does Rabbit use Coyote's cleverness against him?

5. Did any other stories come to your mind when you read this one? If so, which ones?

Social Studies

Make a List This story takes place in the southwestern United States. Look up what states are in the Southwest, and then make a list of them and their capitals.

School-Home Connection Many Native American tales were handed down for years from parents to children. Ask family members whether they know stories that have been handed down from their parents. Ask them to tell you those stories.

Word Count: 1,018